The LITTLE SHEPHERD'S Christmas

The
LITTLE SHEPHERD'S
Christmas

Written & illustrated by

CAROL HEYER

ideals children's books
Nashville, Tennessee

ISBN-13: 978-0-8249-5633-2

Published by Ideals Children's Books
An imprint of Ideals Publications
A Guideposts Company
Nashville, Tennessee
www.idealsbooks.com

Library of Congress CIP data on file

Color separations by Precision Color Graphics, Franklin, Wisconsin
Printed and bound in China

Designed by Katie Jennings

Leo_Jun11_1

For Eloise Freeman, who has always believed in me.

Forever to my parents, William and Merlyn Heyer.

—C. H.

Reuel leaned back and yawned. His favorite little lamb rested against his feet, its soft breath warm and comforting. "Well, little lamb, I better go and join my brothers before I fall asleep." "Baa!" said the baby lamb as it stretched its legs.

Just this morning, his father had finally agreed to let him, the youngest son, come to the fields to work alongside his brothers. If Reuel didn't do a good job taking care of the flock, he was sure it would be a long time before he'd be allowed to return.

Reuel stood up and began to walk among the sheep. "You and the other sheep better listen to everything I tell you," he said to his little lamb.

As he walked, Reuel kept an eye on his brothers. Nagid, the oldest, strutted around like a king watching over his kingdom. His name meant "ruler," and he always tried to boss Reuel around.

His other brother, Amitz, circled the herd, carrying his slingshot. He was always on the lookout for lions or wolves to chase away. His name meant "brave," and Amitz was not frightened of anything.

"Nagid! Amitz! What does my name mean?" he asked.

Amitz laughed. "Your name means 'pest,' little brother!".

Nagid said, "No! It means 'tiny gray mouse that follows his brothers everywhere'!"

Ha! thought Reuel. He'd show them! When he grew up, he'd be braver than Amitz. And he wouldn't *pretend* to be a king, like Nagid. He would be like David—the shepherd boy who grew up to be the ruler of Israel.

Reuel looked up and remembered he was supposed
to be watching the sheep. He turned to check on the
flock and saw that his favorite lamb had disappeared!
"Oh no, where has he gone?" Reuel exclaimed.
The little shepherd grabbed his staff and raced off.
"How could I have been so careless?"

Reuel ran and ran, scrambling down the hill and searching over rocky ledges.

In the distance he heard, "Baa, baa, baa!" He followed the sound, and as he got closer, he saw that the little lamb's fleece was caught in a thornbush.

"There you are!" Reuel untangled the lamb
and hugged it tightly. "I'm so happy you're safe!"
He put the lamb over his shoulders and
started back to rejoin his brothers.

Suddenly the night sky turned bright as day.
The little shepherd shielded his eyes, crying out,
"What's happening?"

Sheep scattered all around him! Nearby, the
other shepherds fell to their knees.

Out of the stillness came an angel who said, "Fear not!
For I bring you tidings of great joy that shall be to all people!"
"Unto you has been born this day in the city of David a
Savior, who is Christ the Lord. You will find the baby wrapped
in swaddling clothes and lying in a manger."
Then a heavenly choir appeared around the angel and
sang, "Glory to God in the highest!"

Reuel couldn't help himself—the music was so beautiful, he sang along: "Glory, glory, glory."

Reuel could not believe he was among those chosen to hear this important message. For surely the child the angels spoke of was the Messiah his people had dreamed of for so long. "We must go to Bethlehem to find the baby!" Reuel shouted.

"Yes!" the shepherds agreed. "The King promised by God has been born!"

Reuel was so excited that he raced ahead of everyone. The young shepherd danced through the city streets, asking everyone he met, "Have you seen the stable with the newborn baby inside?" But they all shook their heads.

Reuel followed the bray of a donkey and the sweet smell of hay to a stable. Inside he saw the baby lying in a manger.

Reuel was happy. He whispered to his lamb, "I'm sure this is the King we seek."

He pushed inside and knelt before the baby, the Savior. The cold night air made the baby shiver, so Reuel laid his little lamb at the child's feet to keep him warm.

The baby opened his eyes and looked straight at Reuel. The young shepherd reached out, and a tiny hand curled around his finger. Reuel knew he was staring into the eyes of the Son of God.

Nagid and Amitz moved forward to stand near their younger brother. Then Nagid said softly, "I finally have the answer to your question, little brother. From this night forward, your name, Reuel, shall mean 'friend of God.'"

Reuel smiled.
He knew this was true.